ΛΙΛΙ ΟΠΗΤΤ

To Laélia, Ulysse, Mila and Marius – H.D.

For my mama... – Q.G.

The illustrations in this book were created using pencils and watercolours.

Hélène Delforge photograph courtesy of Vincent Vandendriesche. Translated by Polly Lawson
First published in French as *Maman* by Éditions Mijade, Namur, Belgium in 2018
First published in English by Floris Books, Edinburgh in 2022. © 2018 Éditions Mijade. Text © 2018 Hélène Delforge
Illustrations © 2018 Quentin Gréban. English edition © 2022 Floris Books
All rights reserved. No part of this book may be reproduced without the prior permission of
Floris Books, Edinburgh www.florisbooks.co.uk
British Library CIP Data available. ISBN 978-178250-771-0. Printed in China through Imago

MIX
Paper from
responsible sources
FSC® C005748

FSC
www.fsc.org

Floris Books supports sustainable forest management
by printing this book on materials made from wood that
comes from responsible sources and reclaimed material

Mama

A World of Mothers and Motherhood

Hélène Delforge

Quentin Gréban

Floris
Books

There will be your first step,
Your first words,
Your first story.
There will be your first swim,
Your first song,
Your first party.
There will be your first friend,
Your first drop of honey,
Your first daisy.
There will be your first giggle,
Your first "Mama!"
Your first "I love you."
So...
Are you waking up, sleepyhead?
A wonderful world is waiting for you.

The miracle: "Mamamamamamama..."
The big moment: "Ma-ma."
The urgent: "Mama!"
The imploring: "Maaaamaaaaa..."
The lazy: "Maaa..."
The possessive: "*My* mama."
The familiar: "Ma..."
The angry: "*Mother!*"
The favourite: "Dearest Mama..."

Will you live on the plains?
Will you sleep under the stars?
Will you drink the milk of the zebu?
Will you paint white clay on your skin?
Will you plunge your hands into the river and into baskets of grain?
Will you be hungry when it doesn't rain?
Will you live outside? Or move to the city?

You are on the edge of worlds:
One disappearing, one self-destructing.
In the middle, find your path.
Protect your love, your happiness,
Treasure the moments,
Know the joy of belonging,
Feel the need to share, and the impulse to laugh,
Find the courage to change.
My daughter, if you hold on to these through each of your days,
If you are true to yourself even within your family,
If you learn to listen and refuse to judge,
Your strength will grow.

My treasure,
My precious,
My miracle,
Stay warm in my strong arms.
Let me, for a few years more,
Be your fortress against the hardships of the world.

My mama said, "I wanted to be a doctor but..."
Then she stopped.
She never finished her sentence.
She was about to say, "I wanted to be a doctor but
    you came along."
My mama didn't study; she raised me.
My mama didn't fight diseases, she soothed my
    scraped knees.
My mama says she has no regrets.
I've always known that's not true.

You came along.
I didn't say, "I wanted to discover the world but..."
I said, "I want to discover the world with you,
    for you, thanks to you."
You're not a brake, you're my engine.
You're not a burden, you're my
    good-luck charm.

"Madam, please cover yourself so you don't offend
    other patrons!"
"Nothing is more beautiful than a mother and her child."
"Are you still feeding that big baby?"
"Doesn't your husband mind that baby always hanging off
    your breast?"
"You mustn't stop before your baby is six months old!"
"That baby is just making a fuss. Let him cry."
"Babies need their mother's milk as long as possible."
"You'd better give him a bottle as well; your milk isn't enough."
"Does the baby always sleep in your bedroom?"
"How are you going to have a life for yourself if you don't stop?"

All these people. All this unwanted advice.
All these words that make no sense.
When you nurse in my arms, the world stops.
I know that all is well;
I hear only your quiet contentment.

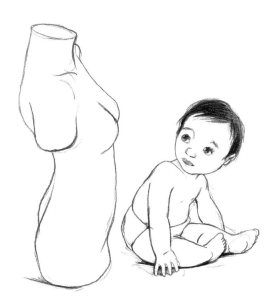

"Stop picking your nose!"

That's right, Mama can see you!
Yes, even when she isn't looking,
Mama can always see you,
Even when you're hiding.
Mama, with eyes in the back of her head,
She's an angel on your shoulder,
Always looking.
Always looking out for you.

And if I startle you,
If I bother you,
If I watch over you,
If I am there, always, sometimes heavy, sometimes light,
It's because
I
am
your mama.
And I *see* you.

"Wipe your nose, smile, we're here!"

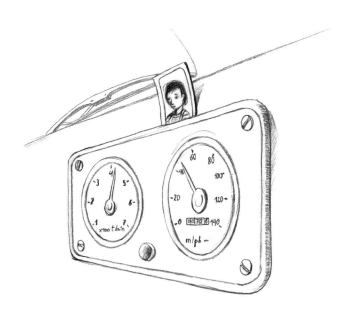

It takes only a few notes
to send babies to sleep
all across the world.
A gentle lullaby,
murmured close, heart to heart.
A steady pulse
to soothe your dreams.
My song is a spell to close your eyelids.
Tucked in my warmth,
in my love,
you sleep.
Me too.
Sometimes me first.

"Do you like my bedroom?" you ask.
"Sweetheart, your baby brother can't see through my skin.
   He doesn't know what your bedroom looks like."
You giggle. "I'm talking about your tummy!
   It was my room first.
   But I've said he can borrow it."

Ever since you felt your little brother move,
He's had all your kisses.
In the morning, when you cuddle up,
You say good morning to him,
Placing your mouth on my skin, humming.
I feel him come to meet you.
He bends himself, curls against your hand,
Gives you a kick in reply.
You tell stories, whisper secrets.

I squeeze you in my arms,
The baby turns towards us:
Three in a hug.

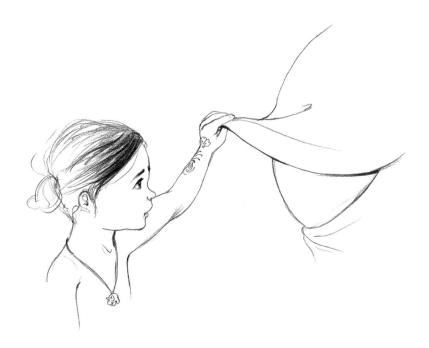

It's an adventure.
You're at the start, I'm close to the end.
You have the world in your hand,
I place mine in yours –
I pass the baton.
An adventure!

Goodbye, new father.
You and I were two,
But now you've gone, and the harvest is all mine.
Life is open wide as the sky.

From today, there's a different two.
At the horizon, a golden light;
In the curve of my arm, the future.
Sleeping.

Little vampires,
Time robbers,
Plan wreckers.
You win.
It was going so well:
You were ready – changed, dressed, clean,
Looking smart for a visit to Grandma's.
I put on my hat and coat.
You opened an eye,
Wrinkled your nose, grizzled.
What? Hungry? *Already?*
And you as well, it seems.
I fed you.
And you.
You fell asleep.
Then you too.
Now it's too late for the visit.
I am tired.

Then you smile.
You too.
Truly, you win, my babies,
because four playful eyes catch mine,
and I'm not angry anymore.

Taking you, collecting you,
Taking you again, collecting you again.
The bus always late, slow, unreliable...
I was so fed up.
On the bus, you would tell me about your day.
We spotted green cars,
We read your school book,
We played 'I Spy'
(you always won).
Sometimes you slept, exhausted.
Now it's past, I miss it.
How could I complain
	that I wasted so much time on the bus?

I promise I'll bring you back peace.
When we meet again,
I'll tell you about the aeroplanes,
About how life is out there,
About teaching drivers to fix their motors,
About helping lost people find each other,
About giving support.
I'll tell you about why I wasn't here.
I hope you'll understand.
I hope you'll understand that being a mother
   is giving an example of how to live,
And that you'll love the one I offered you.

My body was your house.
You lived in me, like a quiet room-mate
    who moved in one night
    and put their toothbrush in the bathroom.
You were under my skin, little one.
Then you moved out.
Signs of your presence remain,
But the house has changed.
I'm empty,
Alone in my skin.
I need to rebuild the house.
Bit by bit, drop of ink by drop of ink,
I create a body in my own image,
Taking back possession of my skin.
I have painted hearts
    on the pink stretch marks you left behind.
I scatter stars,
Birds fly on my back,
An anchor steadies my arm.
I love you.
I am free.
From my head to my toes, I am free.
A new me.
The me I am with you.
Because you are still always with me, child.
Now you're taking up space in my head.

It's funny, we have the same toes.
Big ones and small ones.
We step together,
You cling to my fingers,
You follow my rhythm.
It's what mothers do:
Show the way
   so that their child can walk in their footsteps.
The paths I wander are thorny,
The stones hurt under my shoes.
But you must make your way
   straight towards your desires without detours or mistakes.
I don't want you to go astray.
For you, I need a plan.
And I'll find my way too,
Step by step,
With you.

What do we call a woman who works with engines?
Mechani-tress? Mech-maid?
Mechanic.
I am a mechanic.
I understand machines.
I am a natural.
A naturally skilled mechanic.

Let me tell you a story.
Once upon a time there was a mechanic in a big castle.
She made machines for fairies, to help them fly higher
    than ever before...
Or how about this one?
Once upon a time there was a princess who grew bored
    with watching fencing and jousting.
She decided she would rather work on an engine...

Give me a thousand kisses,
And then a hundred, and then a thousand more.
Rubbing noses, smiling,
Butterfly kisses: my eyelashes, your cheeks.
Airy kisses, tickling your neck,
Secret kisses, light on your forehead,
Ogre kisses, devouring your tummy,
Soft kisses, naughty kisses, sweet kisses on your knees.
What? *More* kisses?
Do you think I have any left?
Maybe.
Just another hundred or so.

My dearest sister, I can't find the words.
Any I try are big, heavy, clumsy,
And yet not weighty enough.
I could say, "Sincere condolences." No.
"Take heart." Virtually an insult.
"I'm here for you." As if that changes anything.
Instead, I put my arms around you.
You ask quietly, dry-eyed:
"Am I not a mama anymore?"
I'm the one who cries.
"You're her mother forever."
"A mama without a child?"
"You'll always be her mama."

In the middle of her day,
A mama offers up a prayer for the little one she
    carries on her back.
Then she starts working again.
The baby stays silent, between warm mama and
    the breezes of life.

Remember that everywhere on this earth
children are held, helped to grow, protected, loved.
Let us take this world full of love
into our hearts.

I promise, all my life,
I'll open my arms when you hurt yourself.
I'll ease the pain with a magic kiss.

And afterwards, I'll put you back on your feet once more.

Ready!
Set!
Go!
Faster than the wind!

One day, I'll be old.
Wrinkles, illness, fading memory: age brings them all.
It doesn't fill me with joy, but I know I can face it.
What's worse is the fear you might not want to visit.
That you'll come out of duty, glancing at your watch.
Worse still, I too might count the seconds,
Impatiently waiting for this stranger, who was my baby, to leave.

Why do I have these thoughts?
Because though you're so little, I'm already afraid of losing you.
It won't happen.
I'll make the most of every minute now;
In them we'll plant the seeds of the hours to come.
Together we'll tend them, and watch them bloom.

My mama

– Q.G.

For mamas everywhere

You don't need to be perfect.
You must be yourself.
You have the right to fail,
    to be exhausted,
And to ask for help when
    you need it.
Does the perfect mother exist?
She does.
She's you.

– H.D.

The creators of *Mama*

Hélène Delforge is a journalist, writer, mother and stepmother. After studying languages and literature at Université libre de Bruxelles, Belgium, she became a teacher and has been a journalist for over twenty years. At home in her native Brussels, Hélène writes overlooking her garden with a cat asleep in her desk drawer and five or six cups of coffee around her computer. She is a parent to four teenagers. *Mama* is her first book.

Quentin Gréban is a world-renowned illustrator and artist. He studied illustration at the Institut Saint-Luc in Brussels, Belgium, and since 1999 has published more than sixty-five children's books, which have been translated all over the world. Quentin won a prestigious Saint-Exupéry award for his picture book *Les contes de l'Alphabet* (*Tales of the Alphabet*). A father of three daughters, Quentin lives in Brussels and works in his home studio, surrounded by drawings of his children and listening to his dog snoring.

The story of *Mama*

Contemplating the work and impact of motherhood, Quentin Gréban imagined a series of portraits of mothers from different cultures and eras. One summer day he showed the work to his sister-in-law and neighbour, Hélène Delforge, a journalist and writer, and asked whether she might be inspired to find words to sit alongside his illustrations in a book. Hélène felt so moved by the portraits that she immediately began writing.

Mama is a unique book born from artistic imagination and from the vivid experiences and emotions of being a mother. Quentin has said that Hélène's words sometimes perfectly mirrored his own ideas of each mama's voice, but just as often there were eye-opening surprises for him.

In *Mama*, Quentin and Hélène set out to create a book that would hold moments of recognition for every parent, carrying feelings and stories both universal and personal. Most of all, they wanted their book to feel real.

Mama has been published in twenty-seven languages; it is loved by readers throughout the world.